Join the Club!

By Megan E. Bryant
Illustrated by Laura Thomas

Grosset & Dunlap

Visit www.strawberryshortcake.com to join the
Friendship Club and redeem your Strawberry
Shortcake Berry Points for "berry" fun stuff!

GROSSET & DUNLAP
Published by the Penguin Group
Penguin Group (USA) Inc., 375 Hudson Street, New York, New York 10014, U.S.A.
Penguin Group (Canada), 90 Eglinton Avenue East, Suite 700, Toronto, Ontario,
Canada M4P 2Y3 (a division of Pearson Penguin Canada Inc.)
Penguin Books Ltd, 80 Strand, London WC2R 0RL, England
Penguin Ireland, 25 St Stephen's Green, Dublin 2, Ireland
(a division of Penguin Books Ltd)
Penguin Group (Australia), 250 Camberwell Road, Camberwell,
Victoria 3124, Australia (a division of Pearson Australia Group Pty Ltd)
Penguin Books India Pvt Ltd, 11 Community Centre,
Panchsheel Park, New Delhi - 110 017, India
Penguin Group (NZ), Cnr Airborne and Rosedale Roads, Albany, Auckland 1310,
New Zealand (a division of Pearson New Zealand Ltd)
Penguin Books (South Africa) (Pty) Ltd, 24 Sturdee Avenue, Rosebank,
Johannesburg 2196, South Africa
Penguin Books Ltd, Registered Offices:
80 Strand, London WC2R 0RL, England

Library of Congress Cataloging-in-Publication Data

Bryant, Megan E.
Join the club! / by Megan E. Bryant ; illustrated by Laura Thomas.
p. cm. — (Strawberry Shortcake's friendship club ; 1)
ISBN 978-0-448-44490-1 (pbk)
I. Thomas, Laura (Laura Dianna) II. Title.
PZ7.B8398Joi 2007
2006019991

10 9 8 7 6 5 4 3 2 1

Chapter 1

Strawberry Shortcake knew exactly what kind of day it was going to be the moment she woke up: cold, gray, and wet! After four days of April showers, Strawberry was ready for a little sun—and so was her cat, Custard. "Oh, I can't bear another day of this rain!" the grumpy kitty complained.

"Good morning to you, too," Strawberry teased.

"Why does the rain bother you so much? I thought you loved sleeping all day."

"I do," Custard replied. "In the *sun*! This rain is too dreary for a cat like me."

"Look on the bright side," Strawberry said cheerfully. "April showers bring May flowers—and May flowers in the berry patch bring June strawberries!"

"Well, there won't be any strawberries if you don't get a chance to go outside and plant your garden," said Custard.

"Oh, but I will," Strawberry said. "And by the time this rain lets up, the ground will be so soft that planting will be easy!"

Boom! A crash of thunder startled them both. Custard dashed under the bed and ran into Strawberry's dog, Pupcake, who could sleep through just about anything.

Strawberry wrapped herself in a quilt and scurried over to the window. "Look at those clouds!" she exclaimed. "The sky is so dark that you can barely tell it's morning. This is the berry worst storm I've seen!"

"And it's probably just going to get worse," Custard grumbled.

"Maybe," Strawberry said. She watched a dark storm cloud glow from a bolt of lightning crackling inside it. "But that doesn't mean we can't have fun today." Strawberry stared at the pouring rain as she tried to think of something fun to do, then turned away from the window. "Come on, Custard. Let's make some breakfast. We'll make this day bright and happy after all—you'll see!"

An hour later, everyone had finished breakfast. "What should I do on this rainy day?" Strawberry wondered. "I really miss hanging out with my friends. Maybe I'll see if anyone wants to come over today!"

Strawberry had been best friends with Huckleberry Pie, Angel Cake, Blueberry Muffin, Ginger Snap, and Orange Blossom for as long as she could remember. Each one of her friends was different—but that only made it more fun when they spent time together. She picked up her phone and dialed Huck's number, but he wasn't home.

Next Strawberry called Angel Cake, who answered her phone right away. "Hi, Angel, it's Strawberry! Do you want to come over today?"

"Oh, Strawberry, I *would*," said Angel. "But it's raining so hard that I'm sure I'd get soaked even if I carried an extra-big umbrella."

"Okay, Angel, I understand," Strawberry said with a smile. "We'll have to get together when the rain stops, okay?"

"Abso-berry-lutely!" replied Angel. "Bye!"

Strawberry dialed Blueberry next, but she didn't want to come over, either. "Sorry, Strawberry," Blueberry said. "But I'm in the middle of a really good book, and I just made some hot chocolate. I'm way too comfy to go out in the rain!"

Luckily for Strawberry, Orange and Ginger were just as tired of the rain as she was. Soon both girls arrived at her bright red strawberry-shaped house.

"You're soaked!" cried Strawberry. "Come into the living room where it's warm and cozy."

"This was a great idea, Strawberry!" Ginger exclaimed as she plopped down on the couch. "The rain was driving me crazy. I tried to come up with an invention to drive away the storm, but nothing worked!"

"It's probably just as well, Ginger," Strawberry said. "All the growing things in the world need this rain. Soon the storm will be a memory, and we'll be able to enjoy the blooming flowers and leafy trees and soft green grass—and berries, of course!— all spring and summer."

"It sounds a lot better when you say it like that," Ginger replied. "That's why I'm especially glad we're hanging out today."

"It's always more fun with your friends— whatever *it* is," agreed Orange.

"Right now I think that 'it' should be making popcorn,"

Strawberry suggested. "Anybody hungry?"

"That's exactly what I was talking about," Ginger said. "Strawberry always has the best ideas!" She and Orange followed Strawberry into her cheery kitchen, where they all worked together—Strawberry made the popcorn, Orange melted the butter, and Ginger sprinkled it with salt.

As she munched on the popcorn, Strawberry couldn't help grinning at her friends. A dreary day became bright and fun—all because they were together.

And that's when Strawberry had another great idea. Her brown eyes sparkled as a smile spread across her face. "Guys!" she exclaimed. "What do you think about starting a Friendship Club?"

"A Friendship Club? What's that?" asked Ginger.

"It would be, like—I mean—it would be a way for us to hang out together even more," Strawberry tried to explain. "A place where we could think up all sorts of cool things to do—like fun projects and stuff! And the best part would be spending lots of time with our berry best friends!"

"I think that's an awesome idea, Strawberry!" Orange replied. "We could have a club motto. And a mascot!"

"And we could build a clubhouse!" Ginger said excitedly. "This might be the best idea you've had yet, Strawberry!"

As Orange and Ginger chatted excitedly about the Friendship Club, Strawberry just had to agree!

Chapter 2

A few days later, Strawberry woke up to the sound of birds chirping instead of rain falling. Sunlight streamed into her bedroom. "I knew the storm would move on!" she exclaimed. "Wake up, Custard! You can sleep in the sun today! And Pupcake, we'll go for a run. You'd love that, wouldn't you?"

"Of course he would," Custard answered for Pupcake. "And I'd love to still be asleep."

"Okay, Custard," Strawberry whispered with a smile. She quietly got dressed and tiptoed out of the room as Custard went back to sleep. Strawberry couldn't wait to meet up with Orange and Ginger to make more plans for the Friendship Club!

After breakfast, Strawberry packed a picnic basket full of yummy food—sandwiches, strawberry tarts, cookies, apples, carrots, and a thermos of lemonade. Then she set off for Ginger's house.

The Berry Trail wound through some of the prettiest parts of Strawberryland on the way to Cookie Corners, where Ginger Snap lived. The tree branches that had been bare just days before were now speckled with tiny green leaves. The sun was warm on Strawberry's back, and she was glad

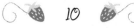

she had remembered to wear her hat.

When Strawberry got to Ginger's house, Orange was already there.

"Strawberry! Hi!" Ginger said excitedly. "I can't wait to show you guys the coolest-awesomest-best plans ever!"

"Let's see them!" replied Strawberry.

Ginger Snap loved inventing and building new creations, and it was obvious that she had put lots of time into her latest design. She unfurled a large scroll of paper.

"Here it is!" Ginger Snap said proudly. "The Friendship Club-house! Up at the tippity-top there's a lookout tower that's high enough for us to see all of Strawberryland. Then there are three layers under it, each one wider than the one above. It kinda makes the clubhouse look like a layer cake!"

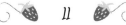

"That's great, Ginger!" Strawberry said.

"But that's just the outside!" Ginger

continued. "Inside, there's the art room—it's got paints and markers and stickers and stuff. The reading corner is in the attic, with big comfy chairs and lots of windows and quiet space to just read or think. And I call this the hangin'-out room—because the only thing it's for is hanging out with friends!"

"Ginger, you outdid yourself," Orange said. "It couldn't be better."

"I agree!" said Strawberry. "It's got everything we could possibly need!"

"I'm so glad you like it." Ginger grinned. "I can't wait to start building! What are we waiting for, anyway? Let's get to it!"

"Hold on just a minute," Strawberry said with a laugh. "There's still one more

big thing we have to decide—*where* are we going to build our clubhouse?"

Ginger and Orange were quiet for a minute. "Good point, Strawberry," Ginger finally said. "I didn't think about that."

"What about the tangerine grove in Orange Blossom Acres?" Orange suggested.

"Or we could build it in Cookie Corners," said Ginger.

"Don't forget Strawberryland," added Strawberry.

"Those are all good ideas," Ginger said. "How are we going to pick one?"

"I bet there are even more places we could build the clubhouse," replied Strawberry. "We can explore all the lands until we find just the right spot. And since we'll be exploring, I know we'll get berry hungry—which is why I packed this picnic."

"All right!" cheered Ginger. "Let's go!"

❀   ❀   ❀

The girls decided to start their search in Cookie Corners.

"Those slabs of cookie-rock would be perfect for building the clubhouse, Ginger," Strawberry said. "But I'm not sure there's a big enough section of flat land to build on!"

Ginger scrunched up her face. "I think you're right," she said. "Let's check out Orange Blossom Acres next."

Orange led the way to her house, which was surrounded by orange, lemon, lime, and tangerine trees. "This is the spot I was thinking of," she said.

Strawberry looked around. She wasn't

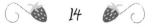

exactly sure where Orange planned to build the clubhouse. The fruit trees grew so closely together that the girls had to walk single file through them.

As if she were reading Strawberry's mind, Orange sighed. "The trees are too close, aren't they?" she asked. "The only way to build a clubhouse here would be to make it a tree house—but Ginger's design is perfect just the way it is."

"Thanks, Orange," Ginger said. "Well, where should we go next?"

"I know a shortcut to Huckleberry Briar," Strawberry suggested.

"We can have our picnic on the shores of the River Fudge!" said Ginger.

Just over the border of Huckleberry Briar, the girls found a sunny spot to have their picnic. Ginger spread a checkered

tablecloth on the ground. Orange Blossom poured the lemonade into cups as Strawberry passed around sandwiches.

"Everything is delicious, Strawberry," Ginger said. "Thanks for making this picnic!"

"I love the lemonade," added Orange.

"Thanks!" replied Strawberry. "I—"

"Hey, look!" Ginger interrupted. She pointed up the hill to Huck's fort. "I think Huck is on the roof!"

"Maybe the storm broke his roof and he's fixing it," Orange said.

"Uh-oh," Strawberry said, frowning.

"Aw, a broken roof's not that bad," Ginger said. "I've fixed them lots of times."

"That's not what I meant," Strawberry said. "I just realized—we've been so excited

about our Friendship Club that we forgot to tell our *other* friends about it!"

Orange's eyes grew wide. "Oh, Strawberry, you're right!" she exclaimed. "I feel awful! I didn't think about it before!"

"Neither did I," admitted Ginger Snap. "That's pretty strange, huh? A Friendship Club without our friends?"

"It doesn't make any sense at all!" Strawberry agreed. "I wouldn't even want to be in a Friendship Club without Huck and Angel and Blueberry!"

"Do you—do you think they'll be mad at us?" Orange asked nervously.

"Of course not!" Ginger said loudly. "How could they be mad? It was just an accident! Besides, it's not like we're leaving them out. We just, uh, started planning it a little bit without them."

"The important thing now is that we tell them about the club right away," Strawberry said. "Let's invite Huck, Angel, and Blueberry over for dinner at my house. We can tell them about the club together."

"Good idea," Ginger said, nodding.

"We should stop looking for a place for the clubhouse," suggested Orange. "It will be better if we all look together."

"Yeah," agreed Ginger. "I know they're gonna be excited about the club, too."

Strawberry hoped Ginger was right—but inside, she was worried. What if the Friendship Club ended up hurting her friends' feelings?

Chapter 3

After the picnic, Ginger went to Huck's house to see if he needed help fixing the roof, while Strawberry and Orange walked home together.

"I think we should have the dinner as soon as we can," Strawberry began. "What about tonight?"

"Sure. If you want, I can call everybody to tell them about it," replied Orange.

"Thanks—that would be great!"

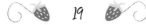

Strawberry said. "What kind of food should we have? Italian?"

"Yum!" Orange said. "I want to have Blueberry's special lasagna. It's the best!"

"Why don't you ask everyone to bring ingredients for a different dish," Strawberry said. "Then we can make dinner together."

"You got it," said Orange as they approached a fork in the road. "This way leads to my house."

"See you later, Orange!" Strawberry said.

But Orange lingered. "Strawberry?" she asked. "Do you think Blueberry, Huck, and Angel will be mad at us for not telling them about the Friendship Club sooner?"

"I hope not," replied Strawberry. "It was an accident, after all!"

A smile spread across Orange's face. "I'm sure you're right," she said. "Bye!"

When Strawberry got home, she took Pupcake for a walk and fed her pets. By the time she was done, the phone was ringing.

"Hello?" Strawberry answered.

"Hi! It's Orange Blossom! Guess what? Everybody can come over for dinner tonight! Is five o'clock okay?"

"That's perfect!" said Strawberry. "See you soon!"

Strawberry hung up and looked around her house. "It's pretty neat in here—but not quite neat enough to have friends over for dinner," she said. "Let's see if I have enough time to get everything ready!"

Strawberry swept the floor and wiped the kitchen counters. Then she set the table with bright red plates. "That looks so cheerful!" she said.

Suddenly, there was a knock. When

Strawberry opened the door, all of her friends were waiting on the doorstep.

"Wow!" Strawberry said with a laugh. "That's good timing!"

"We met up on the way over," Blueberry said. "No one wanted to be late for dinner!"

"Save room for dessert!" Angel said proudly. She was carrying a large pink box. "I made something *very* delicious and *very* wonderful! I'm keeping it a surprise until after dinner!"

In the kitchen, the kids helped get everything ready. Orange tossed a salad, while Ginger poured glasses of milk. Huck made a loaf of buttery garlic bread, while Strawberry and Blueberry made a pan of lasagna. Angel Cake stored her special dessert in the fridge and finished setting the table.

Ding!

When the timer went off, the food was done, and the friends were ready to eat. They sat down together at the table.

"This looks great!" Ginger said.

Blueberry carefully cut large pieces of the cheesy lasagna. "It's really hot," she warned. "Be careful!"

"Orange, would you please pass the salad?" asked Strawberry.

"Of course!" Orange replied.

"Have some garlic bread!" said Huck.

Soon everyone was laughing and chatting as they ate the delicious food. As Strawberry looked around the table, she thought of all the fabulous times they would soon have at the Friendship Club. When she cleared her throat, everyone turned to look at her.

"I have something really exciting to say!" Strawberry announced brightly. "Last week, when it was raining, Orange and Ginger came over. And we had a great idea. We decided to start a Friendship Club—a place where we can have fun together!"

Blueberry, Huck, and Angel looked confused. Then Huck said, "I don't get it. What makes the Friendship Club different from what we're doing right now?"

"Oh, it's totally and completely different!" Ginger burst out.

"Yeah, the Friendship Club is really something special," added Orange. "We're gonna do fun projects and make stuff and—"

"*And* we're gonna build a clubhouse!" interrupted Ginger. "I drew up the best design for a clubhouse you could ever imagine in your whole life! We even went

looking for a spot for it today. That's how I saw you working up on your roof, Huck."

"It sounds like you've already made a lot of plans," Blueberry said quietly.

"Wait a minute," Huck said. He turned to Ginger. "You helped me fix my roof all afternoon and never even once mentioned the club? If we're such good friends, why did you keep it a secret?"

"Oh, Huck, Ginger wasn't keeping it a secret," Strawberry said quickly. "We decided to tell everyone about the club at one time—when we were all together." She bit her lip nervously. Her friends didn't seem excited about the Friendship Club at all—they seemed mad!

"I guess I don't understand why you kept it a secret to begin with," Blueberry said. "You had the idea for a Friendship Club a

25

week ago, and you're only telling us now?"

"No, Blueberry, it's not like that," Strawberry tried to explain. "We just got so excited that we forgot to mention it."

"Forgot? You *forgot*?" Angel's voice sounded shaky. "I don't understand how you forgot about your oldest and best friends, Strawberry! Don't you *like* us anymore?"

"Angel!" Strawberry exclaimed. "Of course I like you. That's why I wanted everyone to come over for dinner tonight. Come on, everybody. *Please* calm down."

But Angel wasn't listening. Her blue eyes filled with tears. "I don't want to calm down!" She gulped. "I can't believe the three of you have this special *club* and we're not a part of it! I hate being left out!"

"Nobody left you out, Angel," Orange spoke up. "It's only because you guys didn't come over to Strawberry's house on that rainy day. If everybody had been there, nobody would be feeling left out."

"I don't see why that matters," snapped Angel. "You couldn't call? You couldn't come visit and tell me about it?"

"Strawberry's right," Blueberry said firmly. "We should all calm down."

Strawberry smiled gratefully at her friend—but Blueberry was looking at Angel and Huck.

"If Orange and Ginger and Strawberry want to have a Friendship Club, that's okay," continued Blueberry. "We can have our own Friendship Club. If they don't need us, then we don't need them."

Strawberry's mouth dropped open. How could her friends *ever* think that she didn't need them? But before she could say

anything, Blueberry, Angel, and Huck had already stood up.

"Sounds good to me," Huck said with a frown. "Since they don't want my help building the clubhouse, I can build one for the three of us."

"No! Wait!" Strawberry cried as she jumped up.

But Angel, Huck, and Blueberry walked out the door.

Strawberry turned back to the table, where Orange and Ginger were sitting in shocked silence.

"Well, that didn't go so well," Ginger said matter-of-factly.

"Not at all," Strawberry agreed sadly. "I guess we should have figured that Angel would be upset. But usually Huck and Blueberry don't get mad like that."

"I don't think they were mad, Strawberry," Orange replied. "I think their feelings were hurt."

"But *why*?" Strawberry asked. "We didn't mean to leave them out. If only they had listened to us—"

"But they didn't," interrupted Ginger Snap. Her dark eyes flashed angrily. "So, fine. If they want to have their own Friendship Club, *fine*. That doesn't get in the way of *our* Friendship Club."

"I guess not," Strawberry said, sighing. "Hey, what are you guys doing tomorrow? I think we should get back to looking for the perfect spot for our clubhouse."

"I'm free!" Orange said immediately.

"So am I," said Ginger. "We need to find a good spot before that other club does. Is anybody still hungry? I am!"

The girls finished their dinner, talking about the Friendship Club and never once mentioning Angel, Huck, or Blueberry. When Orange and Ginger left, the house seemed bigger and emptier than it had that afternoon. It almost felt lonely. Strawberry decided to have a cup of warm milk before bed. It wasn't until she opened the fridge that she noticed Angel's special dessert. They had never found out what it was.

Strawberry peeked inside to find a vanilla layer cake, covered in whipped cream and bright red strawberries. It was one of her favorite desserts— but Strawberry suddenly felt so sad that she couldn't eat a single bite.

Chapter 4

A few days later, Strawberry, Orange, and Ginger were still searching for the perfect spot for their clubhouse. In the Cinnamon Woods, tall cinnamon-stick trees grew closely together, providing cool shade and a spicy smell in the air.

"Yuck," Orange said. "Look at this junk . . . papers, rags . . . is that an old *shoe*?"

Strawberry wrinkled her nose. "That garbage must have blown in during

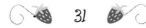

the storm," she replied. "Nobody in Strawberryland would throw trash on the ground!" She pushed through some dense bushes and stepped out of the woods into a small meadow covered with soft grass and clover. A tiny brook of clear water cut through the meadow.

"Oh, wow," Strawberry said softly. "I've never seen this place before. It's beautiful!"

"This is just about the nicest place for a Friendship Club that we could ever find!" Ginger said. She walked along the edge of the meadow, counting loudly.

"What's she doing?" asked Orange.

"I think she's measuring to see how big the meadow is," Strawberry replied as Ginger paced around the meadow.

"Okay! Here's the thing," Ginger reported

back. "I think we can build the clubhouse in the middle. We can build a little bridge over the brook. And guess what? You'll never believe this!"

"What? What?" asked Strawberry.

"The Berry Trail is right on the other side of the field!" exclaimed Ginger. "We took the *long* way getting here, coming through the Cinnamon Woods. We can cut a new path through the field, and it will be even faster to get here!"

"And we can plant a garden outside the clubhouse, too, to make the meadow look even nicer!" said Orange.

"I can already see it!" Strawberry said, her eyes shining happily. "But it's going to take a lot of berry hard work. For starters, there are weeds. Lots of weeds. We

can't start planting until we pull them all."

"The most important thing is building the clubhouse," Ginger said firmly. "All that planting stuff can come later."

"No, it can't!" argued Orange. "Some seeds can only be planted at a certain time of the year. If we miss it, we can't plant them for another whole year."

"Building and planting are both important," Strawberry said quickly before her friends started fighting. "We can do them together. You know what? This gives me another idea. Besides building the clubhouse, we can start our berry first Friendship Club project: giving all of Strawberryland a spring cleaning!"

"What do you mean?" asked Orange. "How do you clean outside?"

"By doing exactly what we're talking

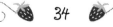

about right now," Strawberry said. "But not just for the meadow and the clubhouse—for everywhere! We can pull weeds and plant flowers and pick up trash, like that junk we saw in the Cinnamon Woods."

Orange slowly nodded her head. "I like that idea!" she said.

"And by the time summer comes, the world will be full of flowers and butterflies and everything beautiful," Strawberry continued. "Besides, we might want to take a break from building sometimes. What do you think, Ginger?"

"It sounds okay," Ginger said. "But how are we going to get the clubhouse ready *and* start a big project like that? We don't have enough people to do it all."

"I know," replied Strawberry. "It would be better if we were working with all our

friends. But since we're not, we'll just have to work berry hard!"

✻ ✻ ✻

Nearby in Huckleberry Briar, the other Friendship Club was having its first meeting.

"Come to order, everybody!" Angel announced. "We have a lot to talk about—starting with figuring out who's going to be in charge of the club. Then we need to come up with a name for our club, and talk about where we should build our clubhouse, and what it should look like, and—"

"You know what I can't wait to do?" Huck said. "Build the clubhouse. When do we start doing that?"

"Yeah," Blueberry said. "Once we have a clubhouse, we can make decisions there."

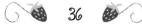

"Oh, *fine*," Angel said. "Let's go find a place for the clubhouse."

The kids set off down the Berry Trail. Suddenly, Angel stopped. "Look!" she whispered. "It's *the other club*!"

Just ahead of them on the trail were Strawberry, Ginger, and Orange!

"Hey!" Huck yelled. "What's up?"

Strawberry looked up. "Oh, hi," she said. "We're just getting started on our first project—spring cleaning Strawberryland!"

"We picked the spot for our clubhouse," Orange added, "in that meadow over there."

"And we noticed that lots of junk had piled up," Ginger finished. "So we figured we could make Strawberryland look even nicer by tidying it up."

"That's a really nice idea!" Blueberry said. "We just started looking for a place to

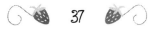

build our own clubhouse."

"That meadow seems like the perfect spot," Huck said. "Good choice."

"Well, I'm sure we'll find just as nice a spot," Angel said coolly. "Come on, Blueberry and Huck!"

Angel walked off quickly with Huck and Blueberry running after her to keep up. "Well, we're just going to have to clean up Strawberryland, too," she said. "Otherwise that *other* club will think that they, like, *own* everything or something!"

Huck and Blueberry looked worried. When Angel got upset, she got *really* upset. Would they be able to calm her down?

Chapter 5

For the next week, both clubs made all the lands prettier. On Saturday, Strawberry, Orange, and Ginger decided to spend the whole day in the Cinnamon Woods.

"Cleaning up the woods is easy and hard," Strawberry said. "It's easy to spot stuff that doesn't belong, like trash. But you have to be berry careful not to disturb the wild animals and plants that live here. Hey—did you hear that?"

"Hear what?" Ginger asked. She and Orange grew quiet, and sure enough, they heard rustling in the bushes.

"Do you think it's a—a bear?" Orange asked nervously.

"Maybe it's a deer," Strawberry replied. "Or—a rabbit?" She held her breath nervously. Then she yelled out, "Hello!"

"Strawberry! What if it *is* a bear?" whispered Ginger Snap.

"Hello?" called a voice.

"It's not a bear," Strawberry replied. "Unless it's a talking bear!" She pushed aside the bushes and came face-to-face with Huck, Blueberry, and Angel.

"I thought I heard people talking," Huck said. "Hi, guys. How are you?"

"We're good," Strawberry replied. "How's your club going?"

Blueberry shrugged. "It's fine," she replied. "Actually, it's—"

"*Actually*, it's better than fine," Angel Cake interrupted. "It's fantastic! We've already started our first project—*we're* picking up trash in the woods."

"Wait a minute," Ginger said as her eyes narrowed. "That's what we're doing! Why are you copying us?"

"We're not!" Angel exclaimed. "You said you were cleaning up Strawberryland. *We're* cleaning up the Cinnamon Woods."

"The Cinnamon Woods are still part of Strawberryland," Orange said. "You just want to clean up the woods because we were cleaning the rest of Strawberryland."

"Nobody owns the Cinnamon Woods," Blueberry replied with a frown.

"Yeah!" Angel snapped. "And since we

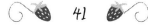 41

were here first, you should just go."

"How do you know you were here first?" Ginger replied. "Maybe we were here first."

"And *maybe* it doesn't matter," Strawberry said, holding up her hands. "The woods are big enough for everybody. We can work in the north part, and you can work in the south part. Okay?"

"Fine with me," Blueberry said quickly.

"Me, too," added Huck. "Come on—let's see if there's trash near the stream."

Strawberry sighed as she watched them walk away. "What's the point of a Friendship Club if we lose some of our friends?"

"It was never supposed to be like this," Ginger said. "But I don't know how to fix it."

"Maybe they don't know how to fix it,

either," Strawberry said. "Sometimes the hardest part of fighting is making up."

"Huck and Blueberry don't seem so mad anymore," Orange said. "But Angel—well, I don't even know how to talk to her!"

"Let's give her a couple more days to cool down," Strawberry suggested. "Then we can try talking to her again."

"By then, I hope we can apologize, and they can apologize, and we can all go back to being friends," Orange suggested.

"I hope so, too," Ginger agreed—but she didn't sound convinced.

The girls spent the next several hours picking up litter and talking about the Friendship Club. Despite spending time sprucing up Strawberryland, they were making good progress on the clubhouse. The first level was already in place, and

Orange had finished weeding a big patch for a garden.

"What time is it?" Strawberry finally asked. "It seems like the sun is setting."

Ginger checked her watch. "It's five o'clock!" she exclaimed.

"I had no idea it was so late," Orange replied. "It's almost dinnertime."

"We'd better go home," Strawberry agreed. "We don't want to be in the woods after dark."

"It's definitely getting chilly," Orange said as she put on her sweatshirt.

"Hey—is that Angel?" Ginger asked, pointing to a clearing off the path.

Strawberry nodded. "I wonder where Huck and Blueberry are." She paused for a moment. "I think I'm going to talk to her."

"Are you sure?" Ginger asked.

"Definitely. See you tomorrow!" Strawberry replied. She walked over to Angel. "Hi," she said quietly.

Angel jumped up, startled. "Oh— Strawberry—what do you want?"

"I thought I'd say hi," Strawberry said simply. "Where are Huck and Blueberry?"

Angel began stuffing more trash into a bag. "They went home a few minutes ago."

"Want to walk home with me?" asked Strawberry. "We can talk, if you want."

Angel's shoulders stiffened. "No thanks," she replied coldly. "I told Huck and Blueberry I was going to keep picking up trash, and that's what I'm going to do."

Strawberry was hurt. "Well, fine," she replied. "See you around—I guess." She walked away, never once looking back.

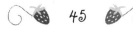

Chapter 6

Strawberry became even more upset with Angel as she walked home. She was so frustrated that she was ready to stop being friends with Angel for good. She told the whole story to Custard and Pupcake.

"And I'm so mad!" Strawberry finished. "I don't understand why Angel won't forgive us—or even talk to us."

"So you're mad at Angel for being mad at you?" asked Custard. "That doesn't

make much sense. How are you going to be friends again if you stay mad at each other?"

"What can I do?" Strawberry asked, throwing her hands into the air. "I didn't pick a fight with Angel. I made a mistake— but she won't forgive me."

"Being mad won't help," Custard said. "All you can do is keep trying to talk to Angel. When she's ready to be friends again, you'll know."

Strawberry sighed. "I guess so," she said.

"You and Angel have been friends for a long time," Custard reminded her. "Everything will work out! It always does for berry best friends."

Darkness was falling when Angel finally

decided to go home. Shadows stretched across the forest floor as the sun slipped below the trees. It was later than she had thought.

Angel shivered and zipped up her jacket. She set off for Cakewalk, but it was hard to tell if she was going the right way. The path twisted and turned, and suddenly Angel came to a fork in the road. She tried to figure out which path led to Cakewalk.

It was impossible to tell. "Left or right?" Angel asked. Her voice echoed spookily in the forest, and suddenly she wanted to be home more than anything in the world.

"I think—I think—left!" she said firmly and charged down the path, following more twists and turns. Nothing looked familiar—the rocks seemed sharp and scary, the trees tall and looming. Was it

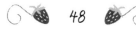

only because she had never been in the forest in the evening—or had she stumbled into a part of the forest she'd never been in before? Angel wanted to be home, *now*, not lost in the woods with no map or compass or flashlight. Suddenly, Angel tripped over a tree root. "Ow!" she cried as she fell. Fighting back tears, she sat in the dirt and examined her scraped hands.

Would she ever get out of the woods?

Back at Strawberry's house, Strawberry ate dinner and thought about everything Custard had said. In her heart, Strawberry knew that Custard was right. She wandered over to the window. In the distance, she could see Angel's layer-cake house. It looked lonely, all by itself in Cakewalk.

"Maybe Angel would like some jam-cakes and vanilla milk," Strawberry said. She marched into the kitchen and started heating a pot of sweetened milk.

"You think she's ready to be friends again?" Custard asked.

"I don't know," Strawberry said. "All I can do is try."

She poured the warm milk into a thermos, put the jam-cakes in her bag, and pulled on her coat. "I'll be back soon, Custard and Pupcake," she promised. "Be good!"

It was now dark in Strawberryland. A silver ribbon of moonlight stretched before Strawberry on the Berry Trail. The air was damp and chilly. It was spooky, being alone in the dark at night.

In a few minutes, Strawberry arrived

at Angel's house. The house seemed just as quiet and lonely as it had looked from her window. Strawberry knocked on the door. "Hello?" she called. "Are you home, Angel?"

No one answered.

Strawberry frowned. It was after dinnertime, and soon it would be bedtime. Why wasn't Angel Cake home? Suddenly, a terrible thought occurred to her.

What if Angel was still in the woods?

Strawberry tried to push the thought out of her mind. "That's ridiculous," she said to herself. "Of course Angel came home! She's probably just visiting Huck or Blueberry."

But try as she might, Strawberry couldn't ignore the thought. She decided that she might as well see if Angel was at Huck's fort or Blueberry's house. She

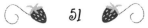

hurried to Huckleberry Briar and knocked on Huck's door.

"Strawberry! What are you doing here?" Huck exclaimed.

"Huck, is Angel Cake here?" Strawberry asked. "She's not at her house."

Huck shook his head. "I haven't seen her since we left the woods."

"Maybe she's at Blueberry's house," Strawberry said. "I think I'll go check."

"I'll come with you," Huck replied, pulling on his coat. "And I'll bring a flashlight. I'm sure Angel's over there."

But Blueberry was home alone, reading a book before bed. She was surprised to see Strawberry and Huck on her doorstep. "I haven't seen Angel since this afternoon," she said, her eyes growing wide. "Do you think she's with Ginger? Or Orange?"

Huck glanced at Strawberry, then looked at the ground. "I doubt it," he said quietly. "She still seemed pretty upset today."

"Well, we might as well check," Strawberry said. "I'm sure we'll find her."

"I'll come with you," Blueberry Muffin said, grabbing her backpack. "And I'll bring a map of Strawberryland and the Cinnamon Woods—just in case we need it!"

The friends didn't have much to say as they rounded the Berry Trail to Cookie Corners. Ginger hadn't seen Angel either, but was quick to join the search—bringing a compass to help them find their way.

Strawberry skipped every other step as she ran up the stairs to Orange's house. She knocked loudly on the door.

"Strawberry! And—and—everybody!"

exclaimed Orange. "What's going on?"

"Is Angel here?" Strawberry asked urgently. "Nobody has seen her since this afternoon."

Orange shook her head. "No," she replied. "Where could she be?"

"I'm afraid she's lost in the woods!" Strawberry cried. "She must be so scared!"

"How will we find her?" asked Ginger. "It's so dark!"

"We can't just leave her there," Blueberry exclaimed. "What are we going to do?"

"We've got to look for her," Strawberry said firmly. "I won't let Angel spend the night alone in the woods—not if I can help it, anyway. Who's coming with me?"

"Me," Huck said.

"And me, too," replied Blueberry.

Orange and Ginger looked at each other.

"We'll help find her," Orange said. "Of course we will!"

Strawberry beamed at her friends. "I *knew* I could count on all of you!" she said.

"Wait a minute," Huck interrupted. "Before we go into the woods, we've got to be prepared. I have a flashlight—"

"And I have a map," Blueberry said.

"I've got a compass," offered Ginger.

"I'll bring a first-aid kit," Orange volunteered. "Just in case."

"And I have drinks and snacks in my bag," Strawberry said. "Is everybody ready?"

"Yes!" chorused her friends.

"Then let's find Angel and bring her home!" Strawberry replied.

Chapter 7

Strawberry and her friends ran to the Cinnamon Woods. All thoughts of separate clubs were forgotten—they had only one goal, and they shared it.

Huck turned on his flashlight, shining a path of light through the darkness. "We have to be careful," he said. "We don't want anybody else getting lost."

"I don't think Angel would stray off the path," Strawberry said. "Let's just start

walking and calling for her." She took a deep breath. "Okay, everybody! Let's go!"

Side by side, the friends marched into the woods, calling Angel's name.

"Angel!"

"Angel!"

"Angel!"

With every step, Strawberry grew more worried. What if they couldn't find Angel?

"Can we stop and rest for a minute?" Orange said. "My legs hurt and I'm tired."

"It's really cold," Blueberry said, shivering.

"We just have to go a little farther," Strawberry said.

"But we've covered almost the whole map," said Ginger. "The only place we haven't been is the Rock Candy Caverns— and I don't know why she'd be *there*."

"Then that's the next place we need to look," Strawberry said. "I know we're all tired and cold, but I also know that if one of us were lost in the woods, Angel would be out here looking—no matter what it took."

The group set off for the Rock Candy Caverns, shouting Angel's name.

"ANGEL!"

Suddenly, a voice called back to them!

"Hello! Help! I'm over here!"

It was Angel Cake!

"Angel!" Strawberry cried. "I'm so glad you're okay!"

The kids ran to hug Angel, cheering and laughing with relief.

"Oh, Angel, you're *freezing*!" Strawberry said as she grabbed her friend's hands.

"Here—wear my coat," offered Huck.

Angel wiped tears off her cheeks. "How did you find me?" she asked. "I thought I was going to have to spend the night in the woods, all by myself! I was hopelessly lost!"

"We'll tell you all about it," promised Strawberry. "But first, let's get you home!"

Soon the kids were in Strawberry's living room, each with a mug of hot chocolate. Angel, wrapped in a big blanket, held out her hands as Orange carefully bandaged them. Strawberry passed around a tray of cookies and cakes.

"Angel, what happened?" she asked. "How did you get lost in the woods?"

"It was almost dark when I decided to

go home," began Angel. "I didn't realize how quickly the sun was going to set. And I didn't have a flashlight or a compass—that wasn't very smart. So I started wandering around in circles, and I tripped—that's how I scraped my hands—and when I realized I had no idea where I was, I decided to stay put until morning."

"That's berry brave," replied Ginger.

Angel shrugged. "Not as brave as all of you coming to find me," she said. "How did you know I was still there?"

"It was Strawberry, actually," Huck said. "When you weren't home she came to our houses to look for you."

"And when nobody knew where you were, Strawberry figured you must still be in the woods," added Blueberry. "So we all joined the search."

Angel Cake turned to Strawberry, her eyes filling with tears again. "Thank you," she said. "I've been really horrible about the Friendship Club, but you've been just as good a friend to me as always."

"You'll always be one of my berry best friends, Angel—no matter what," Strawberry said as she gave Angel a hug. "Besides, everyone worked together to find you."

"When you guys forgot to tell us about the Friendship Club—that really was just a mistake, wasn't it?" asked Blueberry. "You didn't mean to leave us out, did you?"

"Of course not!" exclaimed Ginger and Orange.

"That's what we've been trying to tell you all along," Strawberry said gently.

"Well, I'm convinced," Huck said. "I don't see why we need two Friendship Clubs,

anyway. I mean, if we can still be in your Friendship Club."

"Of course!" Strawberry replied. She looked at Angel. "If you want to."

Angel smiled. "I would love to!"

"Awesome!" cheered Ginger. "We could use some help building the clubhouse."

"I can do that!" Huck said eagerly.

"And I can't imagine painting the walls or making the curtains without Angel and Blueberry," Orange added.

"You got it!" Angel replied.

As her friends started talking excitedly about the Friendship Club—the *only* Friendship Club—Strawberry grinned. It was exactly how she'd wanted things to be!